Peachy and Keen

THE HAUNTED HALLS

by Jason Tharp
and J. B. Rose

SCHOLASTIC INC.

Fellow Dreamer,
Chasing your big dreams can sometimes be
scary. You must believe you are much braver
and stronger than you realize. Don't be scared!
Keep chasing. Keep Dreaming.
You're purr-fect just the way you are.

Be the weiRd YOU want
to see in the woRld!

I believe in you,
Jason

33614080834665

ISBN 978-1-338-27130-0

10 9 8 7 6 5 4 3 2 1   18 19 20 21 22

Printed in the U.S.A.   40
First printing 2018

Book design by Suzanne LaGasa

Contents

A Scare to Remember

"**G**ertie, you have to duck down! He's gonna see your horn through the window!"

Keen the dog and Gertie the unicorn were on either side of a closed classroom door at Happy Tails School, crouched down, waiting. If any of the other students walking, hopping, or slithering by thought this was strange, they didn't show it.

"Are you sure this is the best idea?" Gertie asked Keen, her eyes darting around suspiciously.

"Of course!" said Keen. "I still can't believe you've never heard about the Happy Tails Super Scare-Off."

"I'm still not sure if I *totally* get it," Gertie admitted. "Everyone just takes turns scaring each other? What's the point?"

"It's a tradition!" Keen said excitedly, forgetting to

keep his voice to a whisper. "It starts today and goes until Halloween—whoever pulls off the best scare is the winner!"

"And you think jumping out at Nanner when he leaves his makeup math test is going to win the best scare of all?" Gertie asked.

"Nooo . . ." said Keen, trying to be patient. "We're just getting warmed up! I can't pull out my best scare right away! When Hot Diggity Dog is fighting off bad

guys, he doesn't go to his number-one-super-secret weapon, the lasso made of bacon, right away, does he?"

Gertie had never watched *Hot Diggity Dog*, Keen's favorite TV show, so she wasn't exactly sure how to answer that—luckily, she didn't have to. Through the closed door, they heard a voice say, "Okay, Nanner, time's up! Put down the pencil."

"Shhh!" Keen hissed at Gertie urgently, even though he had been the one talking. "On the count of three," he whispered.

They heard footsteps walking toward the other side of the door. They tried not to giggle as they waited for Nanner. Together, Gertie and Keen counted: "One . . . two . . . THREE!"

"BOO!"

"ARGHHHH!"

A giant gray shape was suddenly flying in the air in front of them. The sound that came from it was so loud that Keen and Gertie were almost scared themselves. The shape jumped so high it clunked against the ceiling before landing back down on the ground. Finally, Keen and Gertie saw what had happened. It hadn't been Nanner walking through the door first at all. Instead it had been—

"Principal Trunx!" Gertie squeaked. "We're *so* sorry! I can't—we didn't—Nanner—we thought—" she sputtered. She was too shocked to form a full sentence.

"We thought you were Nanner," Keen said quickly. In his head, all he could think was: *We are in* so *much trouble.*

Principal Trunx, a large elephant with a large brown mustache and an even larger dislike for Keen and his friends, stared at them. His face was getting very red. Keen wasn't sure if that was from anger or embarrassment. Maybe a little of both. He stood up and brushed himself off.

"And do you usually greet your friends in such a juvenile way?" Principal Trunx asked in a dignified voice.

He stared down his long trunk at them and waited for a response.

"Well," Keen said in a small voice, "it's the Super Scare-Off this week—" Gertie nudged him. She may have been new to this particular Happy Tails Halloween tradition, but even *she* had a feeling that it was probably not a good idea to mention it to their very strict principal.

"Happy Tails School does not support such a thing!" Principal Trunx boomed. "This is a place of learning, not some circus fun house! You're very lucky that I, uh, was definitely not scared at all!"

"Really? I mean, you flew pretty high in the air—" Keen couldn't help himself.

"I was merely giving you an example of why this silly game will not be tolerated," Principal Trunx interrupted. "In a demonstration of how terrified, uh, *some* students could get, if they weren't as clever as me to know that it was coming. I better not see such a display again."

With that, Principal Trunx continued down the hall, giving menacing looks at every student he passed. Gertie and Keen looked at each other in shock for a moment before they burst out laughing.

"Did you see his face?" Keen howled.

"Yeah, sure, he *totally* knew it was coming," Gertie joked. "Just like I'm a magical, imaginary creature. Yeah, right!"

"I'm glad I took my time packing up my books!" said a stylishly accessorized monkey standing in the doorway. It was Nanner, the student they'd been trying to scare all along!

"Nanner! Did you see that?!" Keen said, still laughing. The three friends were doubled over by the doorway, laughing even harder as Nanner reenacted Principal Trunx's reaction, when Peachy the cat walked by on her way to class.

Peachy was Keen's best friend fur-ever. The two pals were also the cofounders of Happy Tails School's first digital magazine, *Purrfect9*. Gertie and Nanner were on the staff of *Purrfect9*, too. Peachy smiled when she saw her friends in such high spirits.

"What's so funny, you three?" she asked.

They filled Peachy in on the whole thing, including more reenactments from Nanner. "And of course Principal Grumps had to make it all serious," Keen added

at the end, "and lecture us about how some students might get really scared—but not him, of course!"

Peachy's smile had disappeared. She gave a nervous laugh. "I mean . . . I think maybe he's kind of right."

"What?!" The other three turned to look at Peachy in shock. "*You're* agreeing with *Principal Trunx?*" Keen asked. "Are you feeling okay?" He reached up to feel Peachy's forehead, but she swatted him away.

"I'm fine," she said hurriedly. "I don't know, I just think maybe he does have a point. You could have really scared Nanner if he had been the first one to come out!"

"Yeah, that's the whole point," Keen said, shrugging.

Nanner nodded, not looking very concerned. "I got lucky," he said with a grin. "But you better watch your tail, Keen! I'll get my revenge! When you least expect it, I'll be lurking in the shadows . . ."

For some reason, Peachy kept glancing over her shoulder nervously. "Look, I'd better go," she said. "I'll see you guys at the *Purrfect9* meeting later!" She darted away before anyone had the chance to respond.

Nanner, Keen, and Gertie stared after her. "Is it just me," Nanner said, "or was Peachy acting very . . . strange?"

Peachy's Secret

PURRFECT9 EMBRACE THE PURRFECT IN YOU!

ater that day, Keen, Nanner, Gertie, and Peachy were together again for their regular *Purrfect9* staff meeting. They were sitting around a table, joined by the other two members of the staff: Connie the octopus, who often wrote about school sports, and Rue the black cat, who covered everything about fashion and style. As usual, Peachy was leading the meeting with some important announcements.

"And so that's why it's best to just avoid questioning a skunk student when he's already irritated," Peachy was saying. "No matter how juicy the story you're reporting is!" She began gathering various papers that were scattered in front of her and stuck her pencil back in its usual spot, behind her ear. "So, I think that's everything

today!" she said to the group. "We can all get working on our next assignments."

"You forgot something, Peachy!" Gertie piped up. "Aren't we going to talk about the Spooktacular? It's only two weeks away!"

"Uh—"

"Oh, yeah!" Keen said, wagging his tail. "We're going to have a booth, right, Peachy?"

"We better!" Connie chimed in. "Gisella keeps going on and on to anyone who will listen—and even some of us who won't—about how 'fantastic' and 'professional' the Drama Club's booth is going to be, and how it will be 'an example of true showmanship' and 'the highlight of the night,'" she said, imitating Gisella the peacock's exaggerated, fancy accent. "We've gotta do something awesome!" Connie was very competitive and didn't like anyone showing her up, no matter what it was for—but especially not for the Spooktacular.

The Happy Tails Spooktacular was the biggest school fund-raiser of the year. All student teams and clubs participated by setting up their own special booths—with a spooky theme, of course. They could sell Halloween treats or put on a show—anything to raise money!

"We can set up a booth to bob for apples!" suggested Nanner. "Or my personal favorite—bob for bananas!"

"Ew," said Rue, scrunching her nose. "Do you know how gross that is? We'd end up with a barrel full of dog slobber."

"Hey!" said Keen, looking offended. Then he seemed to consider it. "Actually, you're right."

"What about a haunted house?" said Gertie.

"That's what the Drama Club is doing," said Connie. "Like I was saying, *fantastic* Gisella told me all about it."

"We could do Halloween face painting," said Rue as she examined her own face from different angles in her compact mirror. "I know how to make it look like someone has guts oozing out of their eyeballs."

"Cool!" said Connie, at the exact same time Gertie said, "Ick, no way!"

"Don't worry, Gertie, I think Art Club is already doing that, anyway," said Nanner. "I overheard a couple zebras talking about it today."

"Peachy, what do you think?" Keen asked, realizing that his usually very chatty and opinionated BFF was suddenly silent. "Peachy?"

She was nowhere to be seen. The group looked around in confusion until Peachy jumped up from under the table.

"Aha, found it!" she said, holding up her pencil. "I, uh, dropped it under the table, silly me. What were you saying, Keen?"

"I was asking what you think about our booth for the Spooktacular," Keen answered slowly. "You always have ideas for this kind of stuff!"

"Yeah, I'm actually shocked you haven't written out an entire plan and assigned us each a job already," said Rue, raising one eyebrow.

Everyone looked at Peachy expectantly.

"Well, I, uh . . . I haven't really . . ." Peachy couldn't seem to get out a full sentence.

"Why have you been acting so weird, Peachy?" asked Keen. "Is something wrong?"

"No, not at—"

BANG. "Aloha, my bodacious beasts!" came a loud voice.

"AHHHH!" Peachy jumped three feet in the air at the unexpected sound behind her. When she landed, she stayed crouched down, hiding behind a chair.

"Peachy, it's just Rocco!" Gertie told her. Rocco was the Happy Tails School janitor and the faculty advisor for *Purrfect9*. He was there to make sure they followed all school club rules—most of the time.

"I knew that!" Peachy shouted, jumping up from behind the chair.

Rue let out a gasp. "I know why you're being weird!" she said, snapping her compact mirror shut triumphantly. "You, Peachy, are a total SCAREDY-CAT!"

Here we have a genuine scaredy-cat!

Mr. Fly's Science Corner

Halloween Heebie-Jeebies

The room was silent.

"Was it something I said?" asked Rocco, still standing by the doorway, looking confused. Everyone ignored him.

Peachy finally responded to Rue. "Don't be ridiculous," she said. "I am most definitely NOT a scaredy-cat."

"Wait, you totally are!" said Nanner, his eyes widening as everything began to make sense. "That's why you were acting all jumpy this morning after these two scared Principal Trunx," he said, pointing to Gertie and Keen.

"And why you said you agree with him about the Super Scare-Off!" said Gertie.

"I can't believe I never knew this about you," said

Keen. "Peachy, we've been best friends fur-ever! Why didn't you tell me?"

As they all looked at her, Peachy sighed. It was no use denying it anymore.

"Okay, okay, you're right," she admitted. "I'm a huge scaredy-cat, and I *hate* Halloween! Things jumping out at you all over the place? Everyone wearing costumes so you don't actually know who is who? Eating so much sugar you feel like you're going to puke? What kind of holiday is that?"

"Who doesn't love costumes?!" Keen shouted. Keen wore a costume every single day of the year.

"I was kind of with you until the sugar part," Connie said to Peachy.

From the doorway, Rocco nodded. "Yeah, it's not a good Halloween unless you have so much candy you feel like you might explode!"

"Well, not for me," said Peachy. "I've never liked it. I used to be better at playing it cool, but that was before coming to school at Happy Tails. The Super Scare-Off makes it way harder to hide that I'm a scaredy-cat. I've been on edge all day!" She shrugged. "Happy now, Rue?"

"Whatever. I don't even like Halloween, either," said Rue. "But not because I'm scared. It's just lame and so gross."

"Says the cat who wanted to use face paint to make fake guts just a minute ago," Nanner joked under his breath.

"It's okay, Peachy," Keen said, putting a paw on his friend's shoulder. "You don't have to like Halloween. And you don't have to help with our Spooktacular booth! You can just sit this one out."

"No way!" said Peachy, eyes wide at the thought. She was never one to *sit out* an important school activity, and she didn't want to start now.

"It's fine!" Keen assured her. "We can come up with something on our own."

"No, Keen, really," said Peachy. "I can't let being afraid stop me from my responsibility to this school and to this magazine! I'm the editor in chief. I'm supposed to be in charge of making sure we have a great booth and raise lots of money."

Here we see the feline in the midst of fight or flight. Look at that determination!

Mr. Fly's Science Corner

Keen didn't look very convinced. "Are you sure?"

"Yes!" Peachy took her pencil from behind her ear and began making notes, looking like her old self again. "And who says our booth has to be scary, anyway?"

"Uh, it is called the *Spook*tacular," Nanner pointed out.

"Yeah, but so what?" Gertie said, wanting to help Peachy out. "I'm sure we can come up with something cool that isn't super scary."

"Gertie's right!" said Rocco, who had finally come into the room. "I predict *Purrfect9* will have the grooviest booth there."

"Predict . . ." Peachy repeated, staring off into space. "That's it, Rocco! We can have a fortune-telling booth! We'll charge students to tell them their futures. We can look into crystal balls and read tea leaves and interpret messages hidden in the stars!"

"All right!" said Rocco. "Can you predict some lotto numbers for me, too?"

"Ooh, and tell me who's gonna win our next football game!" Connie said.

"It will all be pretend," said Peachy with a smile. "But it sounds like . . . you all like the idea?"

"Love it!" Gertie beamed.

"Sounds cool to me!" said Nanner.

"Only if I get to style my own fabulous fortune-teller outfit," said Rue.

"It's an awesome idea, Peachy!" said Keen. "Rocco's right—my prediction is that this booth is going to be a huge hit!"

A Ghostly Rumor

After finally deciding on a fortune-telling booth, the *Purrfect9* staff signed up for after-school shifts to take turns getting the booth ready. The Spooktacular preparations were in full swing at Happy Tails, with students from every club, team, and organization coming to school early or staying late to make sure their booths would be as spook-tastic as possible for the big event. But there was one student who hadn't yet made it to any of her shifts that week.

"I told you, Keen, I was all ready to come help with the booth last night," Peachy said while she and Keen were standing at her locker after first period. "But then I totally forgot that my environmental conservation paper was due today, and I hadn't even started! I had to

spend all night researching which animal's poop is best for composting. Guess which one it is?"

Keen didn't let himself get distracted by this change in topic but made a mental note to ask Peachy the answer later. "You never save papers for the last minute," he said suspiciously. "Are you sure you're not just trying to avoid the Spooktacular? Because you're too scared?"

"Of course not," said Peachy, but she avoided looking at Keen's eyes when she spoke.

Just then, there was a *DING* from Peachy's PinePhone. She pulled it out of her backpack and looked at the screen.

"Hmm," she said with mild interest. "It looks like someone sent an email to the Purrfect Scoop."

The Purrfect Scoop was an email account that Happy Tails students could write to with suggestions for important stories and topics for *Purrfect9*. So far, messages from the Purrfect Scoop had been the inspiration for articles like "Squirrel Away Your Allowance with These Tips from a True Cash Cow" and "Straight From the Horse's Mouth: What Really Happened at the Disastrous Happy Tails Dog and Pony Show."

Peachy scanned the new email on her phone. Keen watched her expression turn from one of curiosity to fright. "What is it?" he asked. Peachy passed him her phone so he could read the email for himself.

TO: PurrfectScoop@HappyTailsSchool.edu
FROM: GisellatheGreat@HappyTailsSchool.edu
RE: GHOST HAUNTING HAPPY TAILS!!

I am writing to report something shocking that you HAVE to share with the whole school on your website!! I have witnessed many suspicious things happen lately that have led me to come to only one possible conclusion: HAPPY TAILS SCHOOL IS BEING HAUNTED. I, like too many of my fellow students, have been at school later than usual working on my club's booth for the Spooktacular. The Drama Club is creating the most fabulous haunted house ever! (Maybe include that in your article. Just, you know, so the students are fully informed and everything.) So anyway, all of us in the Drama Club have been slaving away over this haunted house, because it's going to look super professional, and we've noticed some pretty strange things happening around the school once it gets dark. Things that can't be explained any other way. Purrfect9 has a responsibility to investigate this very serious matter!

Sincerely,
Gisella
Drama Club President
Star of Happy Tails School productions such as The Lion King, Bye Bye Birdy, and Cats

After Keen finished reading, he looked up at Peachy and laughed. "You can't be taking this seriously."

"Why not?" asked Peachy. "Why else would Gisella write this?"

"Because she's Gisella," said Keen. "She loves creating drama! She's literally the president of a club about drama. It says so right here." He waved the screen in her face. "There's no such thing as ghosts, Peachy, you know that."

Peachy couldn't believe that Keen was the one telling her to come back to reality. Usually it was the other way around! "Okay, you're right," she said. "I'm being silly. It's just all this Halloween stuff around me all the time. It makes everything seem way scarier than it actually is! But of course there's no such thing as ghosts."

Peachy hoped she could just ignore Gisella's email and pretend it never happened. But as the day went on, it was clear that would not be the case.

The Purrfect Scoop had never received so many emails in such a short amount of time. Gisella's was only the first. Throughout the school day, Peachy's PinePhone kept buzzing with a new email about the supposed Happy Tails ghost. Students claimed they saw strange shadows in otherwise empty hallways after school. Some swore they heard spooky moaning noises coming from the science wing. Not many seemed to think this was such a joke after all. One student even sent a photo she took of the ghost the previous evening.

"I don't know, that's really too blurry to tell what it is," Connie was saying as she held the photo away from her and tilted her head, squinting. "It's just a blob."

"Yeah, that's usually what *ghosts* look like, Connie: suspicious blurry blobs," Gertie said very seriously.

Some of the *Purrfect9* gang were sitting together at lunch, discussing the latest developments in the ghost stories that were now swirling around the school.

"I can edit the photo in one of my dad's programs and see if we can make out the shape better," Rue said. Rue's dad was the CEO of Calico Computers, and he passed a lot of his handy tech knowledge on to Rue.

"Where's Nanner?" Peachy said, secretly trying to change the subject. "And Keen?"

"I think Keen's in the lunch line," said Gertie, who was still looking at the ghost photo with Connie. "I haven't seen Nanner yet."

Almost on cue, there was a loud commotion over by the lunch line. Everyone turned just in time to see Nanner jumping out from underneath a large pile of lettuce behind the lunch counter, directly in front of Keen. Keen, who had been carrying a cafeteria tray full of food, jumped and threw his tray in the air in surprise, his food flying with it.

"Aha! Revenge!" Nanner cackled from behind the counter, a piece of lettuce stuck behind his ear. His grin disappeared when Mrs. Belle, the cafeteria cow, appeared at his side with her arms crossed. She glared down at him. There was nothing Mrs. Belle hated more than a messy cafeteria.

"Uh-oh," said Gertie. They all watched from a safe distance at their table as Mrs. Belle scolded Nanner.

"So we have to report on this, right?" Connie asked, bringing their conversation back to the ghost as if nothing unusual had just happened. "With so many students writing to us about it, it's clear they're expecting us to look into it and see what's really out there."

"Hold on, Connie, we should wait until after Miss Scaredy-Cat leaves to have this conversation," Rue said with a smirk.

Peachy narrowed her eyes. "I can handle it, Rue," she said.

"Can you?" Rue asked. "Because I heard you still haven't shown up to any of your shifts to build the Spooktacular booth. Wonder why that is?"

"It's okay, Peachy," said Gertie kindly. "We can totally talk about it later."

"Or maybe you should just take a little break from *Purrfect9* while we work on this story," Rue suggested.

"Never!" said Peachy. She was sick of Rue's little jokes and Gertie's kindness was almost worse. She knew Gertie was just trying to help, but she didn't want to be treated like a frail little kitten. She was a mostly grown cat and editor in chief at *Purrfect9*, after all! "In fact," she continued, "I'm going to take on this story all by myself. I'm going to get to the bottom of this and figure out if there really is a Happy Tails ghost. By the time I'm done, that ghost is going to be the one who is afraid of *me*!"

Facing Fears

Yoo-hoo!

Peachy was determined to stick to her word. She insisted on switching shifts with Rue that afternoon so she could finally help out with the Spooktacular booth. After school, she was in the gymnasium with Keen and Gertie. The gym had temporarily been converted into a giant workspace for each club's booth, and it's where the Spooktacular would be held at the end of the week. Peachy tried to ignore the creepy-looking booths from the other clubs that surrounded them.

"Yoo-hoo! Peachy!" Gisella wandered over from the Drama Club's work area. She was carrying a large white sheet with half of a face drawn on it. It looked like she was in the process of making a ghost decoration for the haunted house.

So much for ignoring the other booths, Peachy thought. "Hi, Gisella," she said cautiously, trying to ignore the fake ghost.

"I just wanted to see if you're all looking into this ghost problem," she said. "Not *this* ghost"—she held up the sheet and chuckled. "But, you know"—she looked all around them conspicuously and then lowered her voice to a theatrical whisper—"*the real Ghost of Happy Tails.*"

"Yes, we are," said Peachy in a normal voice. "I am, actually. I'll be investigating it for *Purrfect9.*"

"Oh, fabulous!" said Gisella. "I'm sure you'll need a star witness to interview, and I am more than up to the challenge. I can even work up a few tears if that helps add some emotional interest for your readers." She scrunched up her face and used the ghost sheet to dab at the corners of her eyes to demonstrate.

Peachy heard Keen and Gertie snickering behind her. "Sure, Gisella, we'll call you," she said, hoping that agreeing would get her to go away. "I should really get back to my booth now."

She turned back to help Keen and Gertie, who were gluing gold stars on fancy purple fabric that would be draped all over their fortune-telling booth. "I'm starting to wonder if Gisella totally made up this ghost thing as a trick to get herself into the spotlight," Keen said as they worked.

"What about all the other ghost stories we've heard about, though?" Gertie countered. "From other students?"

Keen shrugged. "They could just be following the herd."

Peachy ignored their ghost talk and got to work. Once she put her head down and focused, she realized it wasn't so bad. Except for the time Louie the rhino jumped out of a garbage can over by the football team's booth to scare his friend, also scaring Peachy in the process . . . but other than that, she was fine. She was even having fun!

After an hour, most students started putting away their craft supplies and were getting ready to go home.

"Ready, Peachy?" Keen asked as he stood up and tried to shake a large amount of gold glitter confetti out of his fur.

"You guys, go ahead," she said. "I just want to finish painting this sign, and then I'll call my mom to come pick me up."

"Okay. See you tomorrow!" Gertie said. And with that, she and Keen went home.

One by one, more students were going home, too, until suddenly, Peachy looked up from her carefully painted sign and realized . . . she was the only one left.

Gulp!

It was pretty creepy being in there all alone, surrounded by the abandoned, half-finished booths. Peachy saw cardboard cutout jack-o'-lanterns, fake spiderwebs, and lots of sheet ghosts staring back at her. It was so silent she swore she could almost hear her own heart beating very quickly.

Okay, calm down, Peachy, she thought. *You're just in the gym at school. You've been here all afternoon. The only difference now is there's no one else around. It's fine.*

She took a deep breath. Her sign was finished, so she could go home now. Or . . .

Or I could stay here a little longer and look for the ghost, she thought.

She knew that's what she should do. She had just told Rue and everyone else at lunch that day that she would find out the truth about this ghost. That's what good reporters were supposed to do: Find out the truth and make sure everyone knew it!

That's what her aunt Priscilla had always told her. Aunt Priscilla had gone to Happy Tails when she was Peachy's age, and she had been the star reporter of the student newspaper (which no longer existed), the *Happy Tails Times*. She had never been afraid to go after a story that could be dangerous—not even when she wrote that undercover exposé about everyday life in a hyena pack.

Peachy stood up, determined. If Aunt Priscilla could do it, so could she! She grabbed her backpack and decided to take a walk around the empty halls and see if she spotted anything fishy (not counting the signs in the halls about auditions for a new all-bass choir).

It was a little creepy being in the empty halls that late, too, but it wasn't so bad. Peachy saw all the usual things that she saw during the school day: lockers, posters advertising the Spooktacular, and the occasional Halloween decoration on a classroom door. Nothing out of the ordinary so far.

She opened the door that led to the science wing. She only made it a few steps when she heard something that made her stop dead in her tracks.

OooooOOOOoooo. Oooooo OOOOOoooo . . .

She heard ghostly moaning noises, just like some students had described in their emails to the Purrfect Scoop! It was faint, but definitely there. Peachy stared down the dimly lit hallway and couldn't see anyone there at all.

"Hello?" she called, but it came out more like a whisper. She slowly crept closer to the noise, moving as silently as possible.

One of the lightbulbs at the end of the hall began to flicker.

FLICK   FLICK

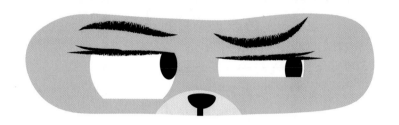

Peachy knew she should keep going. *Ghosts. Aren't. Real.* But no matter how many times she tried to tell herself, she couldn't make her paws move to take another step.

Peaaaachyyyyy . . . Peaaaachyyyy . . .

The voice was suddenly calling her name! *That's it. I'm so outta here!* Peachy turned around and ran back out the door, past the gym, not stopping or looking back until she was all the way to her locker at the other end of the school.

She couldn't believe what she had just heard. It definitely sounded like a ghost, all right. And it knew who she was! But that was just impossible . . . There had to be another explanation. *Too bad I'll never get it*, Peachy thought sadly. She was so embarrassed. What would her aunt Priscilla think? Aunt Priscilla had always been so proud of Peachy, especially after Peachy started *Purrfect9* to be a reporter just like her aunt. But she would never be *just* like her aunt Priscilla, she realized now. She would always be too much of a scaredy-cat.

Costumes and Clues

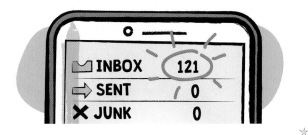

Over the next couple of days, the Happy Tails hallways were buzzing with ghost theories. The Purrfect Scoop inbox was overflowing with messages from students who were convinced they knew the inside story. One student wrote a particularly long and detailed email explaining that Principal Trunx was really a ghost who only took on the form of an elephant as his daytime disguise.

Some students were also starting to leave comments on the *Purrfect9* website, complaining about how they weren't reporting on the ghost sightings. On Gertie's latest article, "8 Tips for Dealing with Your Rowdy Rooster Neighbor When You Just Want to Sleep In," someone had written in the comments: "How can you care about this when there is a GHOST HAUNTING OUR SCHOOL?!

Aren't you supposed to write about things that are important to the students?" The comments got twenty-two "likes" plus one "angry face," from Keen, before Peachy made him change it after explaining the *Purrfect9* staff was not supposed to get into arguments with commenters. Peachy felt horrible. But after her total investigating failure earlier in the week, she had not been able to work up the nerve to try poking around again. She made excuses any time someone asked if she was staying after school to help finish the fortune-telling booth.

"You go ahead," she told Keen at her locker on the last day before the Spooktacular. "All that's left to do is add the finishing touches, and you don't really need me for that, right? I have to work on my article about the ghost investigation."

OMG! GHOST PANIC

"Oooh, how's it going?" Keen asked eagerly. "Did you see anything? Is it really a ghost? Or the real Principal Trunx?" he added with a laugh.

"I'm . . . still conducting the investigation," said Peachy, not meeting Keen's eyes.

"The ghost? I heard it last night!" said a voice. Sheldon, a turtle from the Happy Tails track team, overheard their conversation from his locker across the hall and came over to join them.

"You did?" said Keen. "Where? What happened, Sheldon?"

"I was in the gym working on our booth after school," Sheldon began. "Then I was about to go home, but I remembered I left my bio textbook in class. So I went to the science wing—"

Peachy gasped involuntarily, remembering the horrible sounds she had heard in the science wing a few days before.

"—and I heard it! I had only taken a couple of steps down the hallway and then suddenly I heard this scary moaning and groaning. Then some of the lightbulbs started flickering . . . it was way creepy. I ran to get my textbook super-fast—lucky I'm one of the top sprinters on the track team, or who knows if the thing would've snatched me or something—and I got outta there. Ms. Amino better give me some extra credit for what I had to go through to get my homework done."

"Did it . . . call out your name?" Peachy asked nervously.

"What? The ghost? No," Sheldon said, looking at Peachy strangely. "But that would have been even creepier!" He shook his head and laughed. "If some ghost knew my name, I'd probably never come back to this school again!"

Peachy pretended to laugh, too, as if the idea were ridiculous. But she felt her insides turn to ice. So, other students were definitely hearing the ghost, too—but, so far, no reports of the ghost calling to them by name. It didn't seem like the ghost knew anyone else—except for Peachy.

Great. Just great.

I did it!

MEANWHILE, IN THE FACE-YOUR-FEARS CAVERNS . . .

After two weeks of planning, gluing, cutting, hammering, and glittering, the night of the Spooktacular had finally arrived! The *Purrfect9* crew was almost ready to go, putting the finishing touches on their costumes in the staff room.

Keen had really outdone himself. Since he spent pretty much every day in a costume, he couldn't choose what he wanted to wear for Halloween. So, he had decided to take a little piece of everything: He was wearing a cowboy hat, a pirate eye patch, and a giant red-and-white polka-dot clown bow tie, all over his favorite dinosaur costume. The end result was . . . interesting.

"What exactly are you supposed to be? A total cornball?" Rue asked dryly, looking Keen up and down.

Keen didn't pick up on the insult. "No, silly, I left my corn-on-the-cob costume at home this year. I couldn't get it on with everything else I'm wearing." He looked truly disappointed.

Rue shook her head. She was dressed very glamorously in her outfit for the fortune-telling booth: a big, sparkly purple scarf tied around her head, with lots of gold necklaces, bracelets, and large hoop earrings.

Connie, who was dressed as a giant spider, called out, "C'mon, guys, we better get there before all the good candy is gone!"

"We can't leave without Peachy," Keen said. "Has anyone seen her?"

"She's probably 'sick,'" said Rue, making air quotes with her claws to show that she definitely did not believe Peachy was sick. "So she doesn't have to face Halloween or the ghost."

"I'm here! I'm here!" Peachy shouted, running into the room before they left without her. It had taken long enough to work herself up to attending the Spooktacular with some creepy ghost who knew her name still lurking about somewhere in the school—no way was she going to walk into that gym alone.

"Finally!" said Nanner. He pressed a button on a tiny remote control he had been holding, and the bones on his skeleton costume suddenly lit up and began flashing and changing color.

"Ugh, jeez, Nanner, is that really necessary?" Connie grumbled, squinting as she tried to look in his direction without being blinded.

"Uh, yeah, it is, Connie, how else would I be a Disco Skeleton?" he asked sarcastically, as if this was the most obvious question in the world. "But what's your costume, Peachy?"

Peachy grinned. She was actually very proud of her costume. She was holding pom-poms and wearing a white T-shirt, on which she had written, "Go, Ceiling!" in glittery gold paint. "I'm a ceiling fan!" she announced, standing with her paws on her hips. "Get it? Ceiling *fan?*"

"Clever," said Rue. "I'm surprised you made it at all. Aren't you nervous the Happy Tails ghost might make an appearance tonight, of all nights?"

"Okay, let's do this, everyone!" cheered Gertie loudly, quickly changing the subject. Gertie had decided to use her horn as an advantage for her costume and came dressed as a narwhal. She certainly looked the part!

The Purrfect 9 team made their way through the halls and toward the gym, where they heard loud music and spooky sound effects blaring from the speakers: the sounds of doors creaking, witches cackling, and the occasional scream of terror. Peachy took a deep breath and followed her friends through the doors.

A Spooktacular Night

As Peachy took in the scene, she had to admit—the Spooktacular looked, well, spooktacular! The gym was totally transformed, covered in orange and black streamers, black curtains, balloons, and fake cobwebs. There was a photo booth, face painting, and lots of booths selling all kinds of sugary treats. There was even a booth to bob for apples after all, courtesy of the Happy Tails Horse Alliance. Right in the center of it all (which must have made Gisella very happy) was the Drama Club's haunted house. That was the source of the spooky sound effects, along with a smoke machine and some flashing lights. Peachy noticed they had recruited Gary to serve as their booth's announcer. He was standing in

front of the haunted house entrance and calling out to all who passed by.

"Step right up to walk through the Happy Tails House of Horror!" he boomed. "Only two dollars to get the scare of your life! Enter if you dare!"

"Oh, I dare. Let's go!" shouted Nanner, grabbing whoever was closest to him, which happened to be Peachy and Connie.

"Umm, I don't think so," said Peachy, pulling away. "You couldn't pay me to go in there!"

"Let's go to the cookie-decorating booth!" Keen said, his attention immediately drawn to the snacks, as always.

"That sounds more like my level," Peachy agreed. "Anyone else?"

"I'll come!" said Gertie, flipping her narwhal tail.

"Well, I'm going to check out this haunted house," said Connie. "Let's see if it's really as 'fabulous' as Gisella keeps chirping on about."

Rue had to go straight to the fortune-telling booth to begin giving predictions. Peachy, Keen, and Gertie went to decorate spooky cookies.

They added orange frosting and chose from the many varieties of candy toppings on the table. Ten minutes later, Peachy and Gertie were giggling at how much of a mess they were making when Nanner and Connie joined them.

"That haunted house was FREAKY!" said Nanner, looking positively thrilled.

"Gisella wasn't messing around," Connie admitted. "That *was* pretty cool. And scary! Where's Keen? He'll definitely want to check it out."

Peachy looked around. "He was just right here." The cookies Keen had been decorating sat abandoned on the table.

She and Gertie looked under the table in case he had gone in search of a fallen cookie: no Keen. The friends started looking around at neighboring booths, calling Keen's name. Nothing. *Why would he disappear without saying anything?* Peachy wondered.

"He better not be trying to scare me again," said Nanner, looking over his shoulder suspiciously. "I haven't let my guard down since he got me at the bus stop yesterday."

Suddenly, the music that had been blaring over the speakers stopped. The lively chattering of the many students in the gym lowered to a dull buzz as everyone frowned, wondering what had happened. Then the gym lights began to flicker—until they all went out completely. The only light left was an orangey glow from the candles decorating a few different booths. Someone in the crowd whispered, "The ghost is here!"

Others who heard gasped and Peachy felt like her heart stopped. Was the ghost really, finally going to reveal itself? And was it the reason Keen had suddenly gone missing?

Risky Rescue

Peachy's eyes scanned the crowd, hoping that she would catch a glimpse of a cowboy hat or polka-dot bow tie and realize that Keen had actually been here enjoying himself the whole time. But she still didn't see him anywhere—and then she heard it.

OooooOOOOooooo . . .

It was the same exact sound she had heard in the science wing earlier that week.

"Is that coming from the haunted house?" Gertie asked in a hushed voice.

"No way!" Gisella happened to be standing nearby, her eyes wide in fear. "Our sound effects recording definitely did NOT include any noises like that."

OooooooOOOOOoooo . . .

The sound got louder and louder until every student in the gym had fallen silent, looking all around them to

see where it was coming from. Everyone was frozen, unsure what to do next. Peachy didn't know what to do, either, but she did know she couldn't stand by and do nothing. What if the ghost had taken Keen?

"Hello?" she called out, causing all heads nearby to turn in her direction.

"HelloooooOOOOoo?" the ghost echoed. Nanner's jaw dropped, and Connie clapped four tentacles to her mouth in surprise.

"Peachy, you're *talking to the ghost*," Connie hissed from behind her tentacles.

"What do you want?" Peachy demanded. "Where is Keen? What have you done with him?"

There was a pause, and Peachy wondered if she almost imagined the voice a moment ago. But then—

"Youuuuu'lllll fiiiiind him in the hoooouuuuuse . . ." the ghost answered.

"The house?" Peachy mumbled. "Keen's house? Does it mean—"

"The haunted house!" Nanner said. "Peachy, I think it means Keen is trapped in the haunted house!"

"Huuuuurryyyyy . . ." said the ghost. "Ooooor you'll beeeee toooo laaaaate."

The crowd stared at Peachy. But she wasn't paying attention to them. She was looking at the entrance to the haunted house. She did NOT want to go in there— but if that's where Keen was, trapped and helpless, she had no choice.

"Peachy, maybe there's something else we can do," said Gertie. "Maybe we should go get Principal Trunx."

"There's no time!" said Peachy. "You heard it! Who knows what the ghost might do if I don't get to Keen in time. I have to help him!"

And before anyone could try to talk her out of it— including herself—Peachy turned around and ran into the haunted house after Keen.

It was very dark inside, even darker than the candlelit gym, and Peachy stopped to let her eyes adjust. She tried to ignore the continued moans of the ghost echoing from outside the haunted house and chose one hallway to try first. When she opened the door at the end of it, a giant fake skeleton jumped out at her from the other side.

"AHH!" Peachy shouted, jumping in the air in surprise. "Ugh, get out of my way!" she yelled at the fake skeleton, shoving it aside as she continued looking for Keen.

At the next door, there was no handle—only a sign that said, "Press button here to pass to the next room." The sign pointed to a dark hole in the wall that Peachy couldn't see inside. She couldn't think of anything she would rather do less, but she braced herself and reached her paw in the hole, cringing when she touched something very slimy and cold. Worms?! Guts?! What was she touching? She yanked her paw out immediately and inspected it. *Sniff.* It smelled like—

"Spaghetti?" she said to herself. She put her paw back in the hole and felt around until she hit the button, forcing the door to open.

Peachy pushed past every obstacle the haunted house threw at her: There were a few students in scary costumes who apparently had not heard about what was

happening out in the gym, because they were still manning their posts, ready to jump out at Peachy from behind walls and curtains when she passed by. There was a witch brewing potion, a mad scientist creating something in his lab, and a vampire awakening from his coffin. Peachy ran through it all, frantically searching for Keen the whole time. But when she finally made it to the end of the haunted house, she didn't feel relieved that it was over—because there had been no sign of Keen anywhere inside.

A crowd of students had been waiting for her right outside the exit, including the *Purrfect9* staff. They, too, looked disappointed to see that Keen was not with Peachy.

"You lied!" Peachy shouted into the air at the ghost, wherever it was. "Where's Keen? What have you done with him?"

"You are toooooo laaaate . . ." said the ghost.

Peachy stared at her friends, at a loss for what to do next. As she looked at their faces, she noticed something.

"Where's Rue?" she asked.

"Isn't she at our booth?" said Connie. But when they

all turned the corner to find their fortune-telling booth, they saw that it was completely empty.

"Oh no! Did the ghost get her, too?" Gertie cried out worriedly.

OOoooooOOOOOooo . . .

The ghost was continuing to make noises, and Peachy was finding it hard to concentrate. She began pacing back and forth, trying to figure out where Keen and Rue could possibly be and how she could help them. Then she tripped over something on the ground.

She looked down, puzzled. "Someone bring some candles over here!" she shouted.

Connie ran over holding two candles. Peachy grabbed one and held it over the area on the floor where she had tripped. Something long and skinny was sticking out from behind one of the black curtains hanging around the gym.

"What in the world?" Peachy mumbled to herself. She lifted the curtain aside and gasped.

She was face-to-face with the Happy Tails ghost.

The Moment of Truth

"Rue?!"

The thing Peachy had tripped over was a tail—a tail that belonged to Rue, who was sitting behind the curtain in front of a laptop, speaking into a microphone. Or rather, moaning into a microphone. The microphone was distorting her voice to sound much lower than it really was, and making it loud enough to reach every corner of the gym. She had clearly been the voice of the "ghost" this whole time.

"What's going on?" said a familiar voice over Peachy's shoulder. She turned and saw Keen, who was holding a giant bag of candy. Some of the candy was already stuck in the fur around his mouth, and he looked very confused.

"Keen!" Peachy shouted joyfully, running to her best friend and knocking him over in a hug. "You're alive!"

"Frrmmphh," Keen said, his voice muffled from Peachy's hug and a mouthful of candy.

"Wait a minute. Where did you even come from?!" Nanner shouted. "And what happened to the ghost?"

Peachy stood up and brushed herself off. "There never was a ghost!" she announced, causing murmurs through the crowd. "It was you the whole time, wasn't it, Rue?"

Rue sighed and put down her microphone. She came out from behind the curtain to face the crowd. "Yes," she admitted. "I almost made it to my big finale, too!"

"Wait just a moment!" shouted Gisella, shoving her

way through the front of the crowd. "It was you the whole time? The past two weeks?"

"That's impossible!" declared Nanner.

"Yeah, you've got some explaining to do," added Connie.

"All right, all right," said Rue. "I'll tell you. So, my older sister went to Happy Tails a few years ago, and she told me all about the Super Scare-Off. And I knew I wanted to do something super epic—not those lame so-called scares you've all been doing, jumping out at each other covered in goo or whatever."

"She's not talking about us, is she?" Keen whispered to Nanner.

"I wanted to do something that would scare everyone in the whole school at once!" Rue continued. "So I've been planning this ghost thing all month. My dad let me borrow some of the newest tech equipment from Calico Computers and helped me figure out how to rig the door to the science wing. After four p.m. every day, any time the door opened, it would play a recording I made of 'the ghost' over the loudspeaker. Since the science wing is the closest hallway to the gym, that's where most of you went through when you were done working on the booths. So, a lot of you heard the scary recording and did all the rumor-spreading for me." She shrugged casually. "It was easy, really."

"Wait, wait, wait," piped up Sheldon. "What about the flickering lights?"

"Oh, that," said Rue, waving a paw. "I convinced Rocco earlier this month to hold off on replacing the old lightbulbs in that hallway. Told him it was more festive if they looked a little creepy. They flickered sometimes during the day, too, but it's a lot more noticeable when the hallway is empty and quiet. And, you know, when you already think there's a ghost there."

Peachy frowned. There was still one part of Rue's story that didn't quite add up. "But when I heard the ghost—I mean, when I heard you," she corrected herself. "You said my name! No one else heard their own name, or mine! How did you do that only when I was there?"

Rue broke into a sly smile. "That was a last-minute addition. You told me at lunch that day that you were going to help with the booth and investigate the ghost. I knew you'd be around that night, so I took a chance and switched out the recording to include a new one with your name on it, hoping you'd go down that hallway. Pretty good, right?"

"But, Rue, you said you don't even like Halloween!" Gertie exclaimed.

"That was to throw you guys off my trail," said Rue. "And I can't believe you fell for it. Everyone knows Halloween is the least lame holiday of all! A day all about dressing in fabulous costumes and makeup?" She touched her scarf and fortune-teller jewelry. "How could I *not* love it? That's why I wanted to win the Super Scare-Off. And I would've gotten away with it, too, if it weren't for one meddling reporter . . ."

Peachy suddenly whirled around to look at Keen. "And where were *you* when we all thought the ghost had captured you forever?" she asked him accusingly.

Keen froze. "The cookie-decorating booth ran out of Milky Bones!" he said defensively. "I went to go look for more."

"Yeah, that made my ghost appearance even better," said Rue. "Peachy just assumed I had done something to Keen, so I pretended he was trapped in the haunted house. I never thought you would actually go in there to look for him in a million years."

"You went in the haunted house for me?" Keen asked. "I thought you said you wouldn't go in there even if somebody paid you!"

Peachy looked down at the ground. "Well, I thought you were in trouble," she said, not wanting to make a big deal about it.

Of course Keen wanted to make a very big deal about it. "Peachy! Don't you see? You're not a scaredy-cat at all!"

"But I *was* scared," Peachy insisted.

"You still did it," Keen pointed out. "Because you thought you were helping me. A scaredy-cat definitely would not do something like that, no matter what."

To Peachy's shock, Rue said, "He's right. I was pretty impressed."

Peachy started to blush. "Okay, okay. Well, Rue, I'm pretty impressed with your whole ghost act, too. I totally thought it was real."

"So did I!" said Gertie.

"Me too," said Nanner. He nudged Connie.

"Okay, yeah, me too," admitted Connie.

"And so did everyone in school who wrote messages to the Purrfect Scoop," Peachy added. "So, it sounds like we all agree . . . Rue should be named this year's Super Scare-Off Champion!"

"Aw, man!" Keen said in disappointment while everyone else clapped and cheered.

"You'll get 'em next year, Keen," Peachy told him, stealing a Milky Bone from his bag and popping it in her mouth. "That is, unless this former scaredy-cat gives you a run for your money . . ."

Peachy and Keen

THE HAUNTED HALLS